THE SHORTEST DAY

THE SHORTEST DAY

Susan Cooper

illustrated by Carson Ellis

CANDLEWICK PRESS

So the shortest day came,

and the year died,

And everywhere down the centuries
   of the snow-white world
Came people singing, dancing,
To drive the dark away.

They lighted candles in the winter trees;

They hung their homes with evergreen:

They burned beseeching fires all night long
To keep the year alive.

And when the new year's sunshine blazed awake
They shouted, revelling.

Through all the frosty ages you can hear them
Echoing, behind us—listen!

All the long echoes sing the same delight
This shortest day
As promise wakens in the sleeping land.

They carol, feast, give thanks,
And dearly love their friends,
and hope for peace.

And so do we, here, now,
This year, and every year.

Welcome Yule!

From the very beginning, our lives have been cyclical. At the solstices, the sun reaches its highest or lowest point in our sky, giving us the longest or the shortest day of the year; at the equinoxes, day and night are almost equal. Spring equinox, summer solstice, autumn equinox, winter solstice: round and round they go. If you live on a planet that circles a sun, your time is governed by the patterns of light and darkness, summer and winter, warmth and cold. And, of course, life and death. Once our forebears learned to farm, they planted and harvested at the equinoxes, but it was the solstices that caught their attention. The extremes. They watched their days shrink from the bright abundance of high summer to the bleak, dark cold of winter, and they invented rituals to make sure the light would come back again: to bring the new day, the new year, the rebirth of life.

The rebirth rituals have become traditions that we still celebrate, whether or not we remember where they came from. Some of them are so old that only their monuments remain. On the morning of the winter solstice at the great earthwork Newgrange, in County Meath, Ireland, the day's first beam of sunlight shines in through a passage that Neolithic people built there five thousand years ago to catch it, and for seventeen minutes, a dark room deep within is filled with the sunshine of the shortest day.

It's a universal impulse, this celebration of the light as a symbol of continuing life. The Yule and the evergreens of my poem come from northern Europe, but the candles in those Christmas trees belong to the same family as the menorah candles of Chanukah or the oil lamps of Diwali. Christianity and many other faiths share their intention; they are the lights of hope, reaching for the triumph of good over evil.

The Shortest Day is for everyone. I wrote the poem for the theater, for a joyful celebration of the winter solstice, in music, dance, and words, that's known as the Christmas Revels. (You can find out about it at www.revels.org.) Every year, on Revels stages in nine cities across America, an actor steps forward and begins, quietly: "So the shortest day came . . ." And everybody listening is reminded that above all they too, at this time of celebration, "feast, give thanks, /And dearly love their friends, and hope for peace." So when the actor reaches the last line, the whole audience repeats it after him — or her — in a great exuberant shout: *Welcome Yule!*

The "Jack" of my dedication is the singer-director John Langstaff, who founded the Revels. Its seed was sown in his childhood, when his family always had a big Christmas party for their friends; their house was full of candlelight and good food and evergreens, and everyone sang carols, or played music, or recited a poem.

When your family and friends celebrate Christmas in their own way, maybe you could astonish them all by standing up and reciting *The Shortest Day*. Jack would have liked that.

And the family, suddenly, will be very large indeed.

The Shortest Day ∽ by Susan Cooper

So the shortest day came, and the year died,

And everywhere down the centuries of the snow-white world

Came people singing, dancing,

To drive the dark away.

They lighted candles in the winter trees;

They hung their homes with evergreen;

They burned beseeching fires all night long

To keep the year alive.

And when the new year's sunshine blazed awake

They shouted, revelling.

Through all the frosty ages you can hear them

Echoing, behind us — listen!

All the long echoes sing the same delight

This shortest day

As promise wakens in the sleeping land.

They carol, feast, give thanks,

And dearly love their friends, and hope for peace.

And so do we, here, now,

This year, and every year.

Welcome Yule!

For Jack
S. C.

For my parents
C. E.

First edition 2019

Library of Congress Catalog Card Number 2019939636
ISBN 978-0-7636-8698-7

19 20 21 22 23 24 CCP 10 9 8 7 6 5 4 3 2

Printed in Shenzhen, Guangdong, China

This book was typeset in Bauer Bodoni.
The illustrations were done in gouache.

Candlewick Press
99 Dover Street
Somerville, Massachusetts 02144

visit us at www.candlewick.com